Ladybird books are widely available, but in case of
difficulty may be ordered by post or telephone from:

Ladybird Books – Cash Sales Department
Littlegate Road Paignton Devon TQ3 3BE
Telephone 01803 554761

A catalogue record for this book is available
from the British Library

Published by Ladybird Books Ltd Loughborough Leicestershire UK
Ladybird Books Inc Auburn Maine 04210 USA

The Little
Yellow Digger

by Nicola Baxter
illustrated by Toni Goffe

Bright and early one morning, the Little Yellow Digger went to a big green field.

"I've a Very Important Job for you," said a man, looking at a huge piece of paper. "We need to dig a hole right *here*."

"When there's digging to be done, I'm the digger to do it!" said the Little Yellow Digger. "But can you tell me what..."

"Sorry," said the Man with the Plan. "I'll have a word later. I'm just nipping off for some breakfast."

So with a *clank, clankety clank* the Little Yellow Digger started to dig. Soon he had made a neat round hole and a little pile of earth and grass.

Along came Mrs Macgregor and her little girl Maisy on their way to the shops. "What are you digging?" asked Mrs Macgregor.

"Err ... I don't know yet," said the Little Yellow Digger.

"I do!" said Maisy. "It's a hole for a Giant Flopsy Hopsy Bunny. We'll come back later to see it."

Mrs Macgregor and Maisy went on their way and the Man with the Plan came back from his breakfast.

He looked at the little round hole and shook his head. "I'm afraid," he said, "that the hole needs to be oblong, not round. Keep digging, Little Yellow Digger!"

"That's what I do best!" said the Little Yellow Digger. "But I wonder if you could tell me..."

But the Man with the Plan had gone off for a cup of coffee and a look at his newspaper.

So the Little Yellow Digger started work again. With a *clank, clankety clank* he made the sides of the hole steep and straight. The pile of earth and grass grew as big as a lorry.

Along came Barry, Harry and Gary on their way to school. "What are you digging?" they asked. "Can we help?"

"No," said the Little Yellow Digger quickly. "You have to be *very* good at digging for this kind of work. And... err... I'm not allowed to say what it is *quite yet*."

"I bet *I* know," said Barry. "It's a pond for a fierce Digger-crunching Shinkle Shark. We'll come back after school to see it."

Barry, Harry and Gary went off to school and the Man with the Plan came back from his coffee break. He looked carefully at the hole and shook his head. "It's the right *shape*," he said, "but it needs to be a *lot* bigger! Keep digging!"

"No problem!" said the Little Yellow Digger. "Can you tell me..."

"You're doing a good job! Keep it up!" said the Man with the Plan, looking at his watch. "I'll be back after my lunch."

So with a *clank, clankety clank* the Little Yellow Digger started work again. The oblong hole got bigger and bigger and the pile of earth and grass grew as high as a house.

Along came Daisy and Jim with their dog Tickles. "What is this big oblong hole *for*?" they asked. "Come *here*, Tickles!"

"Err... I'm afraid that's Top Secret," said the Little Yellow Digger. "I really can't say."

"It looks to me as though it might be a trap for a Many-headed Mud Monster," said Jim. "I saw one once on the telly..."

"I *don't* think so, Jim," said Daisy. "We'll come back later to see."

Daisy and Jim and Tickles went on their way and the Man with the Plan came back from his lunch.

He got out his measuring tape and measured all round the hole. Then he shook his head. "It's the right *size* now," he said, "but it needs to be much, much deeper – especially this end! Keep digging, old chap!"

"No sooner said than done!" said the Little Yellow Digger. "Could you..."

But the Man with the Plan had gone off to have a little snooze.

So with a *clank, clankety clank* the Little Yellow Digger started work again. The hole got deeper and deeper and the pile of earth grew as high as a hill.

Along came Sophie on her bicycle, training for a race. "What are you digging?" she asked.

"Well..." began the Little Yellow Digger. But Sophie was already pedalling up the pile of earth. "Don't tell me, I've guessed!" she puffed. "It's for my hill-climbing practice! I'll be back to try it again later."

Sophie whizzed off and the Man with the Plan came back from his snooze. He smiled when he saw the hole.

"This is just right," he said. "But you haven't finished yet, Little Yellow Digger. Look at all this earth. It needs to be carried to those lorries over there and taken away. You're the digger for the job! Keep digging!"

"Just leave it to me!" said the Little Yellow Digger. "Does that mean..."

But the Man with the Plan had gone off to have a cup of tea.

So with a *clank, clankety clank* the Little Yellow Digger carried *all* the earth and *all* the grass over to the lorries. Lots of builders came and started work on the hole. But no matter how much the Little Yellow Digger tried to peep he *couldn't* see what they were doing.

While the Little Yellow Digger was shifting earth, Mrs Macgregor and Maisy came back from the shops. Barry, Harry and Gary came out of school. Daisy and Jim and Tickles came past. And Sophie whizzed by on her bicycle. The Man with the Plan had a quiet word with all of them.

Just as the Little Yellow Digger put the very last scoop of soil into the very last lorry, the builders stopped work as well. Along came the Man with – a great big smile!

"Now that I've finished..." began the Little Yellow Digger. But the Man with the Plan wasn't listening.

"There's one more Very Important Job for you to do," he said. "Hold the end of this banner as high as you can."

With a *clank*, *clank*, *clank* the Little Yellow Digger lifted the banner high above... the brand new swimming pool!

Splish! Splash! In jumped Mrs Macgregor and Maisy. Splosh! In jumped Harry, Barry and Gary...

SWIMMING POOL

and Daisy and Jim and... oh no! Stay *there*, Tickles! Swoosh! In dived Sophie with hardly a splash. And look out – SPLAT! In jumped the Man – without his Plan.

"You kept this secret well, Little Yellow Digger!" they called.

GRAND OPENING